Robert J. Blake

YUDONSI

A TALE FROM THE CANYONS

PHILOMEL BOOKS

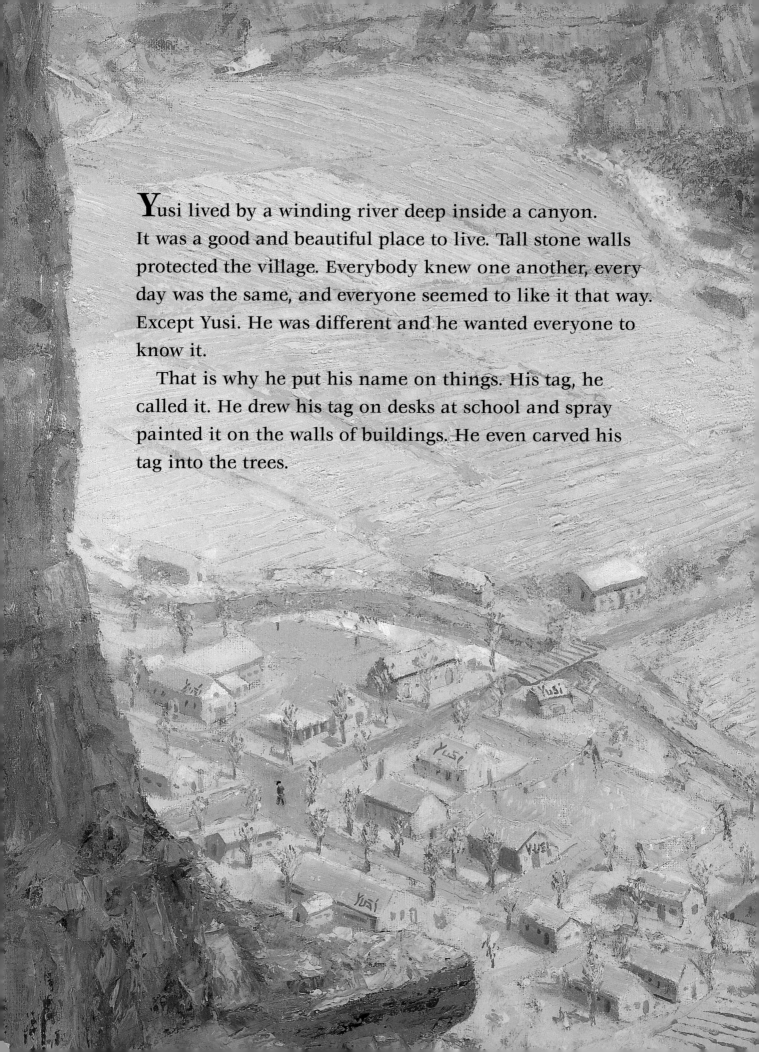

Yusi lived by a winding river deep inside a canyon. It was a good and beautiful place to live. Tall stone walls protected the village. Everybody knew one another, every day was the same, and everyone seemed to like it that way. Except Yusi. He was different and he wanted everyone to know it.

That is why he put his name on things. His tag, he called it. He drew his tag on desks at school and spray painted it on the walls of buildings. He even carved his tag into the trees.

The people thought Yusi's tag made the village ugly. They were concerned that his carving hurt the living trees. For the people believed their whole canyon was alive. They knew the canyon would take care of the people only as long as they cared for the canyon.

They asked the wisest man in the village, Old Wachi, to tell the boy to stop.

"Stop, Yusi," Old Wachi said. "The canyon does not like your tag."

But Yusi would not listen.

So the people decided to ignore him. Whenever Yusi came near them the people turned away. "You don't see," they said to him. Soon everyone came to call him Yudonsi.

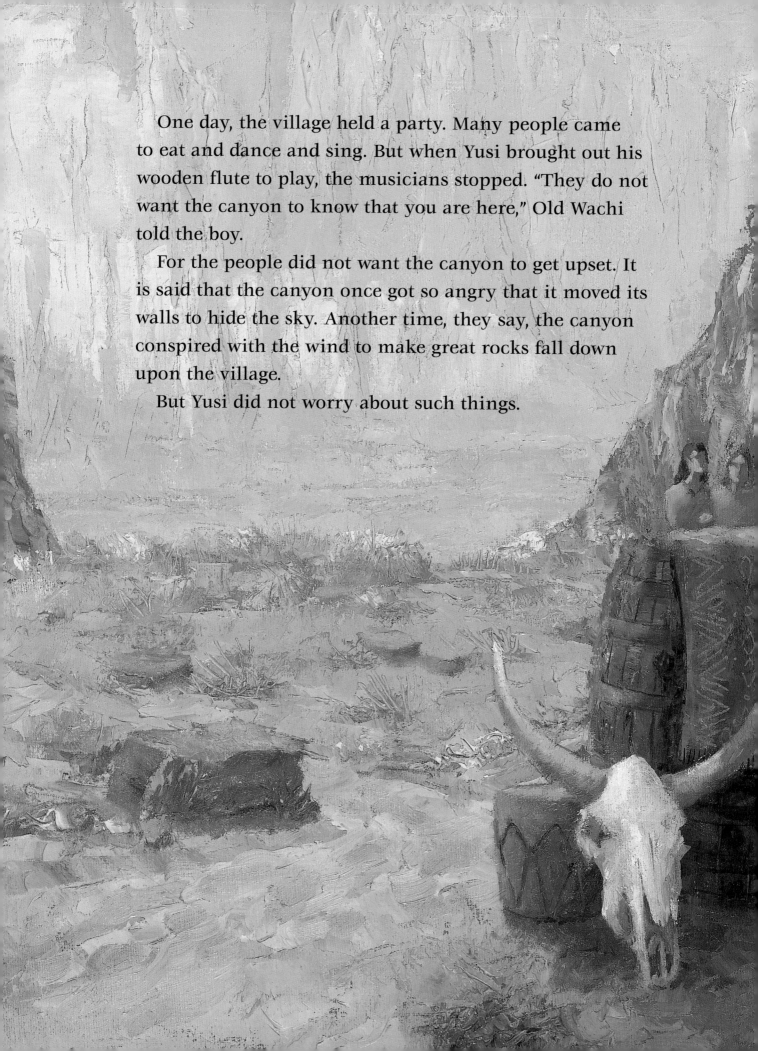

One day, the village held a party. Many people came to eat and dance and sing. But when Yusi brought out his wooden flute to play, the musicians stopped. "They do not want the canyon to know that you are here," Old Wachi told the boy.

For the people did not want the canyon to get upset. It is said that the canyon once got so angry that it moved its walls to hide the sky. Another time, they say, the canyon conspired with the wind to make great rocks fall down upon the village.

But Yusi did not worry about such things.

Yusi wanted to get back at the people for ignoring him.
And so he made a plan. He looked around to find a place
that could be seen from every part of the village. Up high
he saw the long, flat wall that stretched out beneath the
Guardian Cave. That is where he would paint it. The people
could not ignore him if he put his tag up there.

Yusi set off across the river with a pack on his back.

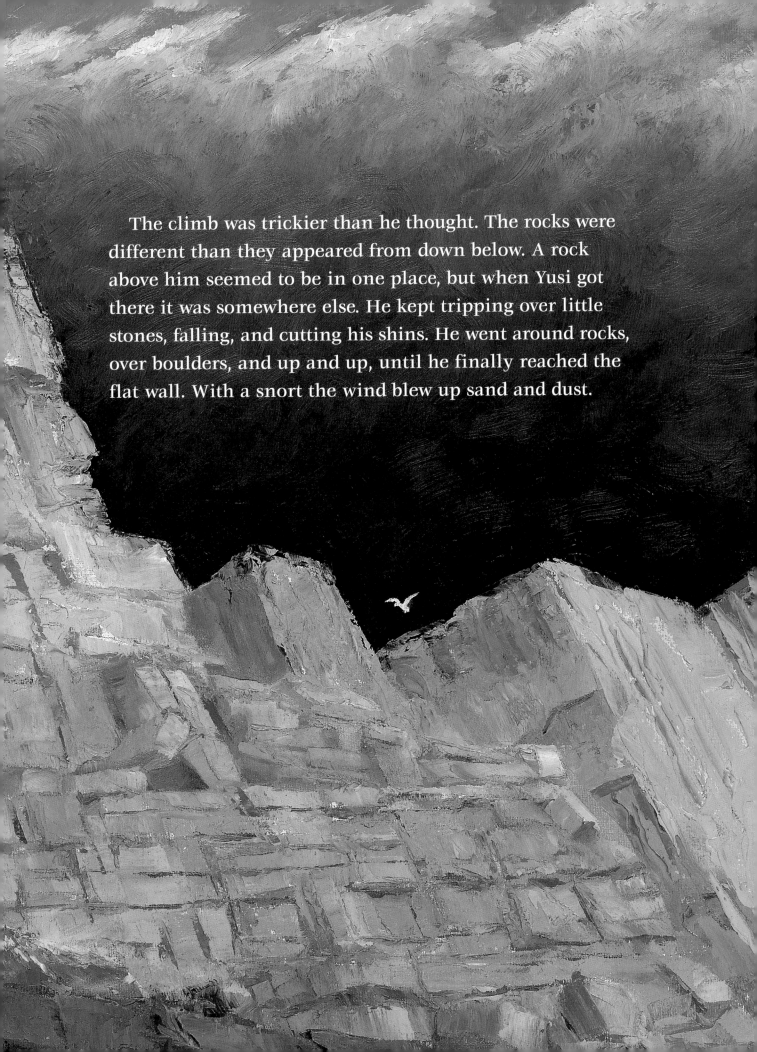

The climb was trickier than he thought. The rocks were different than they appeared from down below. A rock above him seemed to be in one place, but when Yusi got there it was somewhere else. He kept tripping over little stones, falling, and cutting his shins. He went around rocks, over boulders, and up and up, until he finally reached the flat wall. With a snort the wind blew up sand and dust.

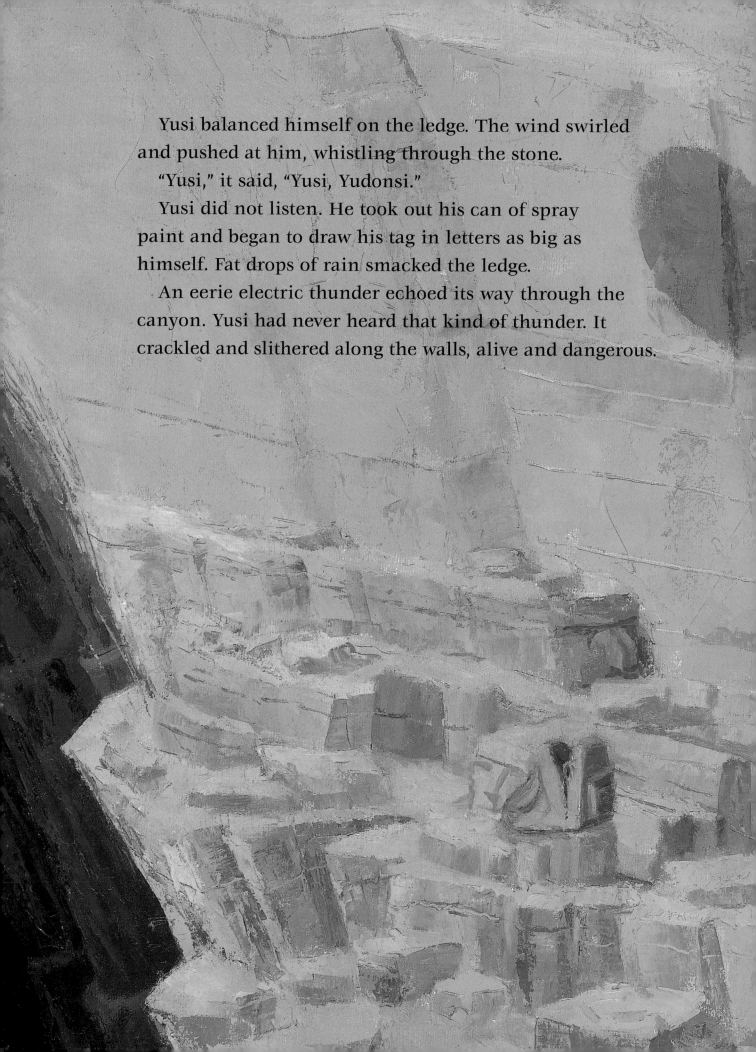

Yusi balanced himself on the ledge. The wind swirled and pushed at him, whistling through the stone.

"Yusi," it said, "Yusi, Yudonsi."

Yusi did not listen. He took out his can of spray paint and began to draw his tag in letters as big as himself. Fat drops of rain smacked the ledge.

An eerie electric thunder echoed its way through the canyon. Yusi had never heard that kind of thunder. It crackled and slithered along the walls, alive and dangerous.

Yusi leaned back to look, and his eyes grew wide. Off to the east, a great gray sheet of rain was rushing down the canyon. Another deafening crash, and the whole world seemed to shift. It was as if the canyon had moved under his feet.

Yusi grabbed for something, anything, as his footing broke away.

His foot caught on a small outcropping. Yusi ran his
fingers along the wall trying to find something to hold
on to as the wind-driven rain poured down on him. He
found an indentation. Then another. Fingertips fighting
for every handhold, Yusi worked his way up and onto the
next ledge.

An ancient rumbling seemed to move from deep within
the earth up to the sky itself. Yusi rolled over and looked
up. A dry cave beckoned him inside.

From inside the cave, Yusi watched waterfalls of rain burst over the plateaus. The canyon was filling up, the village would flood. What about his people? The river would rage, homes would be lost.

Yusi watched, helpless, waiting out the storm.

The daylight grew dim. Yusi turned his ear to the
weather. A pebble kicked, a shuffling sound; something
was coming toward the cave. Quickly, he climbed up
into the cave rocks to hide.

The shadow of Old Wachi fell over the cave.

"Canyon," he said as he walked in, "thank you for
this shelter you have provided for me." The old man
sat down silent, waiting.

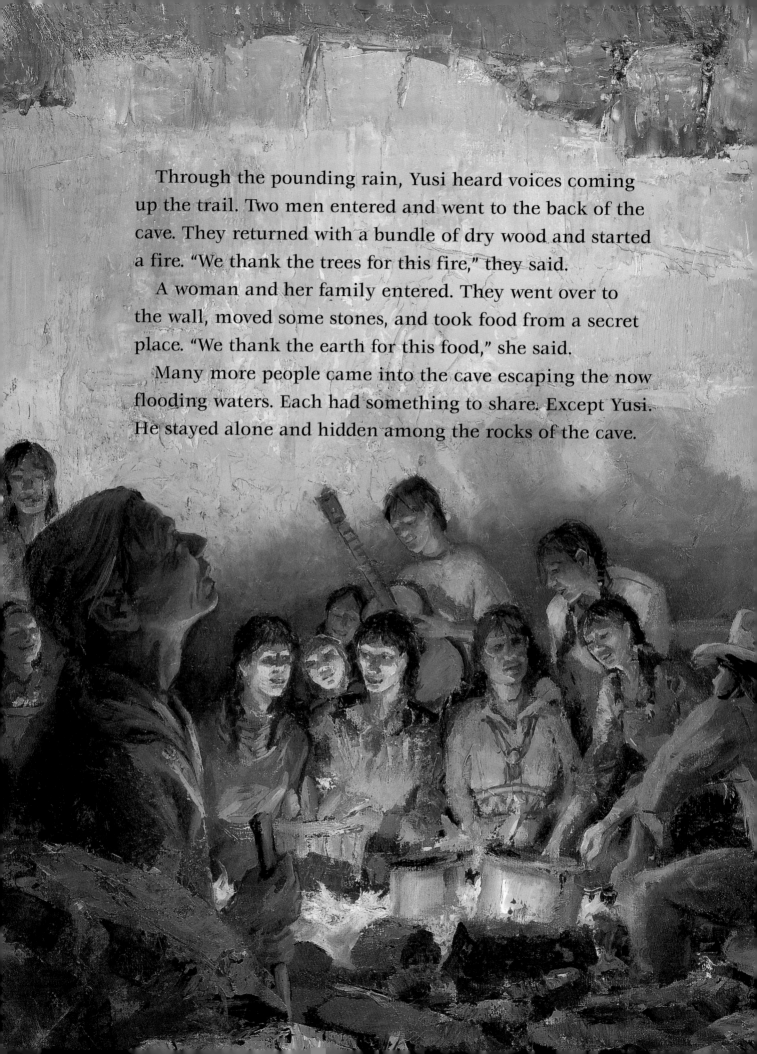

Through the pounding rain, Yusi heard voices coming up the trail. Two men entered and went to the back of the cave. They returned with a bundle of dry wood and started a fire. "We thank the trees for this fire," they said.

A woman and her family entered. They went over to the wall, moved some stones, and took food from a secret place. "We thank the earth for this food," she said.

Many more people came into the cave escaping the now flooding waters. Each had something to share. Except Yusi. He stayed alone and hidden among the rocks of the cave.

From high overhead Yusi watched the people. He saw their joy as they ate and played and shared. He leaned back and breathed in the rain and the fire and the very cave itself, until the smells and the sights and the sounds all wove together.

He began to understand.

Everything is a part of everything.

Yusi took a deep breath and raised his flute.

The music moved not from him, but through him.
He played a song that he had never heard before.
And the people heard it and joined in the song. For
when Yusi played, he played with the timeless spirit
that all things share.

Later the people would say that the sky cleared
the moment Yusi began his song. They'd say the
walls came alive with the song of the ages.

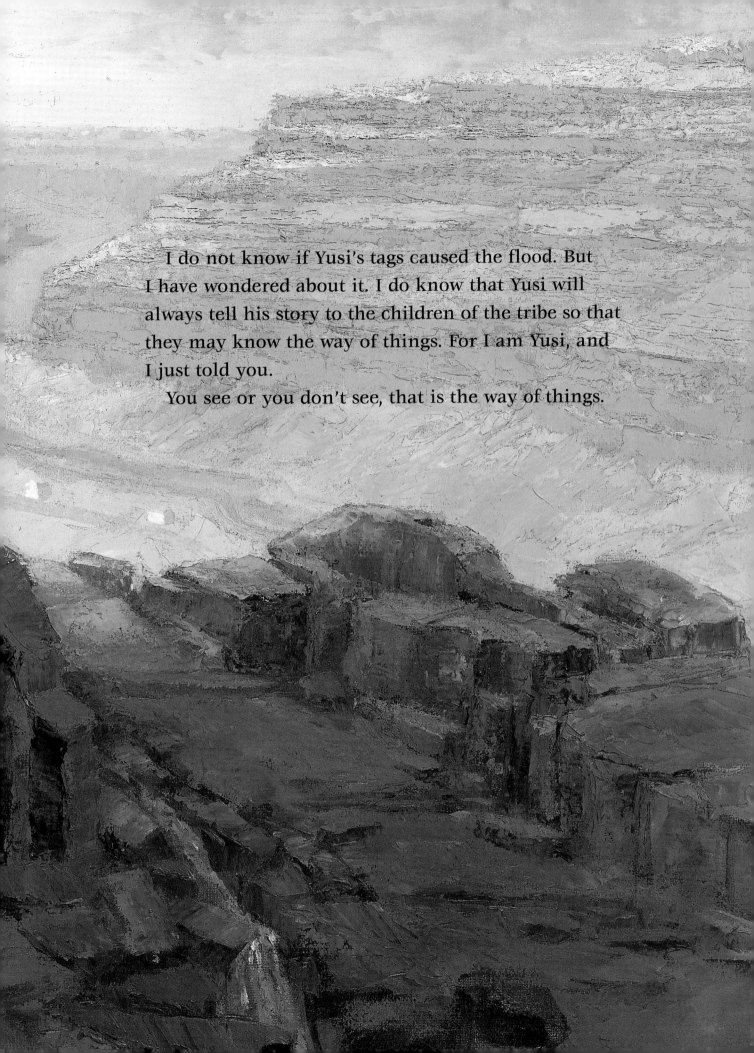

I do not know if Yusi's tags caused the flood. But I have wondered about it. I do know that Yusi will always tell his story to the children of the tribe so that they may know the way of things. For I am Yusi, and I just told you.

You see or you don't see, that is the way of things.

To my second-grade teacher, Ms. Motichka:
You made a difference.

ALSO BY ROBERT J. BLAKE:

The Perfect Spot
Dog
Spray
Akiak

WRITTEN BY FRANCES WARD WELLER:
Riptide
The Angel of Mill Street

To create the story and art for *Yudonsi* I traveled across the canyon lands of the
American Southwest. I would like to express my appreciation and respect to
the many people who talked with me as I wrote and painted in my sketchbook.

Patricia Lee Gauch, editor

Text and illustrations copyright © 1999 by Robert J. Blake. All rights reserved.
This book, or parts thereof, may not be reproduced in any form without permission in writing
from the publisher, Philomel Books, a division of Penguin Putnam Books for Young Readers,
345 Hudson Street, New York, NY 10014. Philomel Books, Reg. U.S. Pat & Tm. Off.
Published simultaneously in Canada. Printed in Hong Kong by South China Printing Co. (1988) Ltd.
Book design by Donna Mark. The text is set in Veljovic Medium.

The art for this book was created with oil paints on canvas using a palette knife.

Library of Congress Cataloging-in-Publication Data
Blake, Robert J. Yudonsi / by Robert J. Blake   p.   cm. Summary: Yusi wants people
to notice that he is different, so he puts his "tag" on desks, walls, and even trees,
alienating everyone in his village. [1. Indians of North America—Southwest, New—Fiction.]
I. Title PZ7.B564Yu 1999 98-33755 [e]—dc21 CIP AC ISBN 0-399-23320-2
1 3 5 7 9 10 8 6 4 2
FIRST IMPRESSION